Down By the Creek
Ripples and Reflections

Down By the Creek
Ripples and Reflections

by

Paul Stansbury

Sheppard Press

Sheppard Press
461 Boone Trail
Danville, Kentucky 40422

Printed in the United States of America
ISBN 978-0-9986516-0-6 paperback
ISBN 978-0-9986516-1-3 eBook

Cover Graphics by Paul Stansbury.

Cover Photo: Fern Creek at Stansbury Lane, Fern Creek, Kentucky.
This is the real site of "The Old Rotten Bridge".

Editorial assistance by Joan Stansbury, affectionately known as the
"Queen of Commas".

Table of Contents

Introduction

I have been writing for some years because it provides me a creative outlet. I write about anything that strikes my fancy, so people who read my work have learned to expect almost anything. The only caveat I have is any member of my family should be comfortable reading something I have written.

As a child in the 1950's, I grew up in Fern Creek, Kentucky, between the suburbs of Louisville and the farms that then existed in Jefferson County. There, my Grandparents, George and Frances Stansbury, had purchased a little over twelve acres of farm land just before the outbreak of World War II. Fern Creek meandered around two sides of the property. Woods covered a generous portion of the higher ground.

They moved out from the city to their new home with their two sons, Edward and George. Edward was my father. Both saw action in the Pacific Theatre during World War II; thankfully, they returned home safely to establish their own lives on the family property. They married their wartime sweethearts and built their lifelong homes on the property alongside their parents. They raised their children - my generation - and lived out their lives. Two of my cousins have also built homes on the property, firmly establishing the homestead.

Down By The Creek is a collection of tales and reflections influenced by my experiences growing up in this setting.

Paul Stansbury

Fishing Down By The Creek: Ripple One

If you grow up by a creek, you just have to go fishing. It's the fifth fundamental law of the universe. And really, that one sentence could pretty much serve as an introduction to my first story. I think it's important to point out that fishing can teach you many things: patience, appreciation of quiet time, perseverance, respect for nature, and sharing, to mention a few. There is no guarantee, however, that every time you throw out your line, you will learn one of these life lessons, as you will find out from this story. But, anytime you go fishing, you're bound to learn something.

"Of Bullies And Bobbers" is loosely based on my experiences while fishing on Fern Creek. Of course, I have incorporated the necessary embellishments to flesh out the story and create some humor.

In fishing, a "keeper" is a catch fine enough to take home. If you learn only one thing from fishing and this tale, it's that the most important "keeper" is the experience, not the fish.

Of Bullies and Bobbers[1]

Now, I'm not one to wish ill towards people or to take delight in the misfortune of others, unless of course it's a politician, lawyer, TV evangelist, or cousin LJ. I guess most folks would understand about the politicians, lawyers, and TV evangelists because I don't hear hardly anything good about them from anyone. Of course, Aunt Earlene does think highly of TV evangelists. But I don't put much stock in what she believes by the fact that she thinks the sun rises and sets in her son, cousin LJ. The truth is that most everyone else who ever met him would just as soon see a rainy day.

The thought occurs that you may not have met LJ and be curious or even dismayed at my attitude toward him. (I'm sure you agree with me on the others!) LJ was three years older than me, a fact that he never failed to bring up when we were together. He was also the oldest in our generation of relatives and for some unknown reason, although I think Aunt Earlene had a lot to do with it, he believed it gave him the right to order the rest of us around like his personal servants. Even that wouldn't have been so bad had he not been a liar and bully to boot.

Now, I don't plan to tell you all the things that LJ did to us and how he made life miserable for me. I don't have the time nor the inclination to write that much. You'll just have to believe me when I tell you that he generally treated me and his other siblings and cousins very poorly. You see, LJ relied on his age and size to boss us around. And even though LJ planned and orchestrated most of the mischief we got into, we couldn't tell on him for fear of getting beaten up. More times than I care to remember, LJ coerced me into some unsavory

---

[1] "Of Bullies and Bobbers" was a Mayfest '95 (Lexington, Kentucky) selection.

5

activity that ended with me getting a good whipping while LJ lied his way out of it.

Yes, I'd have to say that LJ was a pure bully, not the slick and devious kind of bully that politicians, lawyers, and TV evangelists are. Not that they are any less effective in their bullying than LJ. It's just that they use different methods, ones less readily recognized as bullying. Misinformation, deception, big words, and lawsuits are their bullying tools. For my money, if I must be bullied, I prefer it the way LJ did it. You knew what to expect and he never let you down.

But, I'm getting too far from what I was going to tell you about. As I said earlier, I don't generally take delight in the misfortune of others. There was one time when I did, and to this day, I still do and quite frankly, I don't feel the least bit sorry for it.

I guess I was about 11 or 12 when it happened. My family, my grandparents, and LJ's family lived on several acres out in the country. A slow moving creek ran through the property. I'd say it was about 4 feet at its deepest and that being after a good rain. Most of the time it was 2 to 3 feet deep. This was back when creeks weren't filled with the runoff from shopping centers or Bud Light cans or dirty needles. You could actually wade in it and feel the soft muck squeeze up through your toes without fear of getting cut on broken glass or rusted appliance parts.

The creek was a center of attention for us. Whether it was skipping stones, catching crawdads, or racing sticks under the bridge, it seemed that almost every summer day would find us there. And of course, there was fishing, our most important activity. As you can guess, 'specially if you have done any fishing at all, we each had our special spots and secret places along the creek where we would fish, believing that these held the brightest bluegill and fattest catfish.

One particular stretch of the creek had a regular bridge at one end and a dilapidated footbridge at the other. About 50 yards of creek lay in between. Here, walnut trees lined the banks. They were so big, two of us couldn't reach around and clasp hands. Lilies sprung up in bright orange shocks. The ground was covered in wild violets and it smelled like the arboretum in the park. Crawdads built their battlements on the mudflats and water bugs danced on the ripples. The creek was about 25 feet from bank to bank and the limbs of the trees reached across the water to each other, providing a shady canopy over the water. This kept it cool even on the hottest days and the water looked dark and murky in the shade.

This was a favorite fishing place, especially on hot days. And it was on one such summer hot day that I gathered my fishing gear and headed down to the creek. When I got there, I spied LJ on the opposing bank with his fishing gear. He seemed to take little notice of me until I baited my hook and prepared to cast. Just as I drew back my Zebco 25 to plunk a line in a favorite hole, he called out to me to get away from his fishing place and forbade me to poach his area. It usually took 2 or 3 three threats before LJ would take action, so I decided to test the waters and casted out. It wasn't two seconds after the bobber settled that I got a strike and reeled in a feisty bluegill.

Of course, this did not go unnoticed by LJ, who wasted no time in letting me know that if I didn't clear out immediately, he was going to come over and let me have it. By this time, I had baited and cast out again. As soon as the bait hit the water, I had another bluegill on the line. LJ was fit to be tied. He had just finished cussing me a blue streak when I pitched my bait about 5 feet from his. Sure enough, the bobber barely had time to settle before I hooked another fish. Even though LJ was about 35 feet away, I could tell that his tolerance level had been used up and that he was buzzing into action.

Like any good fisherman, LJ wouldn't leave his pole with his line out so he began to furiously wind his reel. Likewise, I did the same. He started up the bank to the regular bridge with hate in his eye and mayhem in his heart. I knew I couldn't stay there, otherwise, he would make good on his promises to inflict all manner of bodily harm on me. In a straight run across the fields to the house, I guessed that he could easily run me down, so I figured that my best bet was to head down the creek to the old footbridge. Here I had the advantage, being smaller and sure-footed, and figured that I could easily beat him across the rickety footbridge and have the safety of the water between us.

Sure enough, just as I thought, I was able to get across and back up the opposite creek bank while LJ wobbled slowly across the swaying footbridge. Just about the time LJ got off, I was up at the regular bridge ready to cross. I could see the wheels turning in LJ's head. He knew I had him over a barrel.

No matter which way he went, I had an avenue of escape which allowed me to keep the creek between us. He would try to come up the creek bank and I'd cross the bridge to the other side. Then he would start back across the footbridge and I'd linger where I was, then drift back down the bank when he reached the other side. Sometimes we'd be directly across the creek from each other, LJ cussing, and me smiling.

After about 5 minutes of this cat and mouse game, we were back where we started. LJ was livid, and it wasn't about fishing any longer. He had taken it to a higher plain. His authority had been challenged and his ability to enforce it thwarted. As for myself, I realized that one, I'd eventually have to make a break for the house, and two, sooner or later, I'd have to face LJ. It was just at this moment when the unexpected happened.

LJ took about 2 steps back from the creek bank and made a running dive into the creek heading straight for me. My heart fell to my knees and lay there twitching. I had not planned on LJ's resolve or his resourcefulness. LJ was on the high school swim team and had worked as a lifeguard at scout camp. I knew that he would be across the creek in a flash and upon me before I could reach either bridge or the house. Like a frog caught in the search light, I stood paralyzed, waiting to be gigged.

What emerged from the creek about 10 feet away was not at all what I expected. At first I thought it was old Slick Belly. That legendary catfish was rumored to be so large that it could swallow a dog and so heavy that its belly was slick from dragging around on the creek bottom. The thing I saw lifted its black, slimy head and turned two large flat eyes toward me. They, too, were black. I thought LJ had been swallowed alive.

It wasn't until after the creature stood up and removed its glasses, revealing pink-rimmed eyes that I realized it was LJ. The water was not as deep as he thought when he dove in and he had stuck his face in the black muck that covered the creek bottom. This was the kind of muck that the early settlers prized after the spring floods deposited great stretches of it along the creek banks. It was so rich; you could grow a bushel of corn in a thimble full. Its dark, pungent odor reached my nose in only a few seconds.

The fire had gone out of LJ's eyes. It had been replaced by a forlorn gaze and tears left pink trails down his cheeks. He wiped a wet hand across his face, scraping off a swath of sticky mud. He wretched and opened his mouth, ejecting a huge wad of muck and half of a front tooth with his tongue. He coughed and spat several more grey wads of mud and saliva before he climbed up on the bank.

I stood ready for the beating of my life. Instead, LJ walked slowly past me and on to his house. He had retired from the battlefield. I had finally gotten the best of him, even though he had really done it to himself. Nonetheless, you take a victory whenever and however it comes.

Now, I have had the satisfaction of seeing a few politicians, lawyers, and TV evangelists get their comeuppance. I do believe, however, nothing before or after was quite as funny and satisfying as seeing LJ spit out that wad of muck. I think we all need to see our bullies get their wings clipped once in a while, otherwise we might just give up hope. Even now, the memory of old LJ spitting mud and climbing out of that creek brings a smile to my face. I never told anyone what happened and I guess for that reason LJ never did seek revenge. Besides, I wanted to keep it just between him and me 'cause sometimes seeing a bully get his comeuppance is sweeter when you know he's got to worry about other folks finding out the real story.

Of course, LJ didn't stop his bullying because of this, but afterward, it seemed I caught a whole lot less of it. The one thing I do know, however, is that we never argued over fishing rights again.

End

Looking Back: Reflection One

The Old Rotten Bridge[2]

Do you remember it as I do,
The Old Rotten Bridge and what it meant to you?

Arrrrrrrrrrrrrrrrrr Matey, 'twas the plank on our pirate ship,
Where we'd sail all day long at a mighty clip.

It stretched to the rock where I wouldn't go,
Because snakes lived there, so said Jo.

Stopping midway to fish was a pleasure,
Then on to the rock to bury our treasure.

Do you remember it as I do,
The Old Rotten Bridge and what it meant to you?

As long as we knew it was falling apart,
In time, crossing it grew to be quite an art.

We threw our sticks in the creek with a wish,
Watching them race underneath with a swish.

Over the old cedar logs we would march,

---

[2] Inspired by conversations with my dear cousins: John Stansbury, Jessica Stansbury, Hannah Stansbury Schardein, Jo Danielle Stansbury, Jessica Evans Leep, Judy Stansbury Leep, Jennifer Jo Stansbury Sawchak, & Jim Stansbury. The war mentioned refers to World War II.

Out to the rock, through the rough wooden arch.

Do you remember it as I do,
The Old Rotten Bridge and what it meant to you?

Granny would sit there - writing letters to each son,
Praying they'd return once the war was won.

Fished there with Dad when he caught a big turtle,
But it spit out the hook and disappeared with a gurgle.

Down below, 'neath the rotting expanse,
I knew in the murk, the beasties did dance.

Do you remember what it meant to you?
That Old Rotten Bridge, I hope you do!

Pranks Down By The Creek: Ripple Two

"Boys will be boys," so goes the saying. I must confess it is true and many of our experiences down by the creek would prove it. One of the many ways boys will be boys is by playing pranks on each other. It must be another law of the universe. Most pranks are merely some trick of an amusing or playful nature. Sometimes not. Unfortunately, boys being boys often lack the fine sensibility to tell the difference.

"How He Got His Nickname" is another tale loosely based on my experiences. It tells of a prank that failed and succeeded at the same time. How could that happen, you ask? Well, you judge the failure or success of a prank based on your level of involvement and how its final outcome affects you. I can't say it much simpler than that, but if you're still unsure, you'll just have to read this story and figure it out for yourself.

How He Got His Nickname

This is a story of a prank that backfired. It happened when I was about 11 or 12, which I hate to say was quite a while ago. We lived on a bit of land that started where a small stream ducked under Watterson Trail and flowed into Fern Creek. It continued on until it spilled over an old dam into the adjacent country club's golf course. A gravel road almost two football fields in length paralleled the creek and served as our driveway.

It's a wonder my father didn't go broke replenishing the gravel that we eagerly confiscated to throw in the creek. Boys and rocks, it must be in the genes. Flat rocks were prized for skipping contests. Smooth, round stones were valued for the mesmerizing "plunk" sound they made when thrown straight up, allowing them to plummet vertically into the water. Why we didn't fill that creek up with rocks, I'll never know. We also had a flat field on the other side of the road. It was always referred to as the "bottom". It was the site of many a pickup baseball and football game.

As far as I know, that was one of the very few spots along the creek providing easy access to the water as well as some flat playing area. A bunch of us about the same age lived in the area and as you might well guess, that sweet ribbon of water was a natural gathering place. Many days, we would gather along its banks to practice the now arcane art of playing in the creek. If that didn't suit us, we could always play ball in the "bottom".

On a sultry, August day just about two weeks before school was to start, Shorty Evans, Buzzy Riesman, Pudgy Lumpkins, and I were tossing walnuts through an old tire we had propped up against a tree. Shorty was all of 4 feet tall. Buzzy always had a buzz haircut because once a week his dad clipped his hair GI style. And as for Pudgy . . . well, Pudgy was pudgy.

We were down at the lake end of the creek and could see Brad Bates across the expanse of water. He was loading something into a boat. We all did a double take when we realized it was not his old, beat-up olive drab skiff, but a bright, shiny, aluminum john boat none of us had ever seen before. We watched Brad for a while as he carefully loaded the boat.

"Whachyadoin?" Shorty yelled out.

Brad continued without so much as giving Shorty a nod. After a while, he climbed into the boat and shoved off. We watched as he paddled a short distance from the shore and dropped something over the side of the boat that made a big splash when it hit the water. Then, he paddled a bit further and tossed something out which bobbed up and down in the soft ripples of the lake. He made his way across, tossing more items out at regular intervals until he had almost reached our side of the lake.

"Hello, losers." Brad called out, as the boat nosed up to the bank.

We could see the smirky grin on his face that meant he was going to say or do something to show his self-imagined superiority. He placed the paddle inside the boat and threw us a line to tie off. He stepped forward over the seats and neatly on the bank.

"Well, what do you think?" he asked, gesturing to the shiny, aluminum boat. Not waiting for a reply, he continued, "It's the Fisherman's Friend. The newest and most expensive fishing boat Fern Creek Marine has on its floor. Cost $65, not including the paddle."

Buzzy, who was not readily impressed, pointed out across the water and asked, "Whacha throwin' in the lake?"

Peeved more by the fact that Buzzy didn't demonstrate proper awe over his new boat, rather than the question itself, Brad mustered up a cold stare and answered from between clenched teeth, "It's a trotline, stupid. You tie one end of your line to a big rock and toss it in. Then every few feet or so you tie a cork float and dangle your hook and bait from it. When you get to the other end, you tie on another rock and pitch it in the water. Then, you can go do what you want. When you come back, you just yank the fish right in your boat. Now if you don't mind, I got two more lines to set before I toss the rock in."

"Can I ride in the boat?" Shorty asked, as Brad started to step off the bank. Slowly, Brad turned and rolled his eyes.

"Look, I can't waste my time giving boat rides to losers. I told you I had to finish up with my trotline." With that, he placed one foot in the boat but hesitated. "Well, mebbe we can work somethin' out. What say one of you comes up with something really good and I'll let you finish up for me. That way you can ride in the boat and I can take a rest. What do ya say?"

It took all of two seconds for us to start digging through our pockets to find something to trade for a ride in the boat. I fished a Bob Gibson rookie card from my shirt pocket and offered it up.

"Naw, he'll never amount to nothing." Brad said with disdain. "You'll have to come up with something better than that if you want to get in my boat."

Shorty dug his hands in every pocket he had but came up empty. Buzzy pulled off his shoe and retrieved a nickel. "It's an Indian head, 1938 and in good shape, too."

"Still only worth five cents." Brad replied, dismissing Buzzy with a flick of his hand. Then he looked Pudgy square in the eye, almost daring him to offer something. "You got anything, big boy?"

17

Pudgy stood there for a moment staring at Brad. Because of his size, other kids were reluctant to let Pudgy ride their bikes or try out "new" stuff. Slowly, he slid his hand in the front pocket of his shorts. His hand lingered there for a moment before he pulled out a Sugar Daddy, pristine in its bright yellow and red wrapper. Pudgy held it gently with both hands, stretching out his short arms with the offering.

Brad stared at the Sugar Daddy. We all stared at Brad. Finally, he pointed right at Pudgy and shouted, "That's what I'm talking about! Hand it over big boy and you can hop in the boat."

Pudgy stared at the Sugar Daddy. We all stared at Pudgy. We knew that he rarely departed with anything he could eat. He started to pull it back, then asked in a plaintiff voice, "All by myself?"

"Sure thing."

Before Pudgy could react, Brad reached out and snatched the candy. Pudgy's face had a look of excitement and sadness. After all, while he was going to take the Fisherman's Friend out all by himself, he was losing a good candy bar.

We stood on the bank for a short time while Brad explained all the rules to Pudgy. "Don't get mud in the boat. Don't splash water in the boat. Don't eat in the boat. Don't mess with the tackle box. Don't go too far. Don't stay out too long. Don't stand up."

Pudgy patiently nodded at each rule while alternately glancing at the shiny new boat and the Sugar Daddy. Finally, after Brad had run through the list a second time, he pointed toward the boat.

"Whacha waitin' for? I don't have all day to waste on you. Get going or get out of the way!"

We steadied the boat at the water's edge while Pudgy carefully stepped in. The bow sunk right down as his weight transferred from the bank to the boat. For a moment, we thought it might go under, but

Pudgy continued to move toward the back of the boat and it regained its balance. Reaching the last bench, Pudgy turned to face forward and sat down. The bow was now riding high in the air and we could only see Pudgy from his shoulders up. A broad smile beamed across his face. He picked up the paddle as we gave the boat a shove and watched as it floated away from the shore.

Brad peeled the wrapper off the Sugar Daddy and we could smell its caramel sweetness. We sat on the bank watching as Pudgy paddled out and dropped the last two lines. Then, he tied the end of the trotline to one of the remaining rocks and hefted it over the side. We sat in the shade under the low hanging trees and enjoyed a cool breeze working its way around the shore. Out on the lake however, the sun beat down on Pudgy and we could see him wiping his forehead as he paddled around.

It wasn't long before Pudgy slowly turned the boat in our direction and began to make his way back to shore. The closer he got, the more the bow obscured our view. First, it covered his knees, then his lap, then his belly. We stood up in preparation to help him out when he got to shore. He had stopped again, puffing from all the paddling, to wipe his forehead and suck down some hot air. Just then, Brad fished something out of his back pocket.

"Watch this. It ought to be fun."

What happened next was totally unexpected. Brad stood with his hand behind his back, grasping a rubber snake. Pudgy had just paddled close enough that we could only see him from his shirt pockets up over the bow of the boat.

"Look!" Brad shouted, pointing to a spot in the lake behind Pudgy, who immediately craned his neck around to see what it was. We also looked, being fooled by Brad's ploy. As Pudgy's head was turned, Brad tossed the rubber snake into the bow of the boat making

19

a little "thunk" sound when it landed. This grabbed Pudgy's attention and he snapped his head back to the front. For a split second, nothing happened. Then, Pudgy sat bolt upright, eyes about to pop out of his head and we realized he had seen the snake.

We started to laugh, and to be honest, I thought Pudgy would whoop and holler, spew out a few choice cuss words and that would be it for a harmless prank. Boy, I was wrong.

Before Brad could get the "Wai" of "Wait" out of his mouth, Pudgy, not known for his speed or agility, rose full up from his seat in one single, fluid motion. There was no stumbling, no fumbling – only the swift, calculated movement of a fine athlete. He had grabbed a large rock from the bottom of the boat which he raised high above his head. His burning eyes stared down in front of him, face fixed in cool determination. Looking every bit like Charlton Heston's Moses, he stood ready to unleash his wrath. With all the force in his body, he cast down the stone, which landed with a wrenching thud. The sound of tearing metal echoed over the lake.

We looked on in stunned silence. Pudgy stood motionless, his eyes riveted on the front of the boat. Then, imperceptibly, the bow began to rise. Slowly, it blocked more and more of our view. At the same time, the rear of the boat began to sink. We could hear the rush of water over the transom. We watched as water engulfed the boat. Faster and faster the stern went down until the lake surface was chest high on Pudgy. Water continued to roll over the sides of the hull until, at last, the boat leveled out and softly sank beneath the waves.

Still, Pudgy had not moved. Yellow Cheetos crumbs jettisoned from his shirt pockets, briefly whorling around him before they drifted off in the slow moving current with the other debris cast off from the boat. The severed front and back halves of the rubber snake bobbed happily as they were carried away.

No one had said anything. Pudgy gazed up at us. His eyes had the look of complete satisfaction and contentment. The current gradually carried away the muddy swirls kicked up when the boat hit bottom and we could see the bright, shiny hull resting on the lakebed with Pudgy still standing in the stern.

Shorty, never at a loss for words, turned to Brad and said in his best deadpan, "Well Commodore, there goes the fleet."

Hot tears leaked out from the corners of Brad's eyes and without a word, the Commodore turned, head hanging, and walked off. We turned our attention to Pudgy, who by now was regaining some motion. He gingerly stepped along the sunken hull until we could reach his hands and we pulled and tugged for all we were worth until we had him safely up on the bank. For a few minutes, we just stood there looking at the boat beneath the water. Buzzy spied the tie off line floating along the bank and reached down to retrieve it. With nothing to lose, we decided to tug the boat up on shore. After even more work that it took to get Pudgy on dry ground, we finally released the boat from its watery grave.

We looked and looked for a hole in the boat. We turned it over and examined every seam and rivet. We didn't even find a dent. Flipping it back, we saw the severely mangled tackle box. Suddenly, it all became clear. Pudgy's rock had hit the tackle box and not the boat. It sank because he had stepped back when he stood up, causing the stern to dip below the waterline. We looked for the Commodore to tell him; but by this time, he was almost to his house and out of earshot.

We paddled the boat back across the lake and hid it in the bushes below the Commodore's house. We didn't tell him for a day or two, just to let him stew in his own juices. We owed that much to

Pudgy. When we finally told the Commodore, he was so mad and happy at the same time he was speechless.

Well, now you know how the Commodore got his nickname and how a "harmless" prank sank a boat. It seemed to me after that, Brad behaved more like a regular guy – he didn't act so superior, especially when Pudgy was around. Of course, we didn't stop playing pranks completely, but it seemed they never again quite reached the heights of the rubber snake incident and they sure happened fewer and further between. Whether that was from a lesson learned or just the natural result of growing up, you'll have to be the judge. Oh, and if you're curious what my nickname was and how I got it; well, that's another story altogether.

End

Looking Back: Reflection Two

Dedifferentiation

Would that I could walk once again
Down dirt paths to the water's edge
In child's shoes, worn and soft.

Play hide and seek with sunbeams
Under nature's green thatched umbrellas
Held high by trees older than my grandfather.

Sip nectar from honeysuckle blossoms
Lining the old, rutted, gravel road
Where rocks scrunched under bicycle tires.

Skip stones across the still pond
Splashes appearing like fairy footsteps
Disappearing at its far edge.

Climb the tallest tree
Perched on the hill's crest
Surveying my kingdom below.

Run through fallow fields
Tall fescue sweeping under my chin
Collecting burrs on pant legs.

Make forts of old limbs
Soft dry leaves spread on the floors
Hiding from enemies unseen.

Lie on breezy hillsides
Cool grass brushing my cheek
Watching clouds saunter by.

Listen, deep in the thick woods,
For goblins' mournful songs
While sitting still and silent.

Would that I could see once again
Wonders once never seen before
Through child's eyes, inquisitive and naive.

Love and Romance Down By The Creek: Ripple Three

For adolescent boys, romance along the creek was a remote if not completely missing aspect of life. Then, as we grew up and floundered between adolescence and senior high, we experienced those brief moments when our heads were turned by the opposite sex. When this happened, the creek could prove a handy backdrop. A nice, clean creek was impressive to most young ladies and I think young suitors would certainly recognize the opportunities a walk along the creek bank could provide. I cannot really point to any particular experience I personally had down at the creek, but it is safe to say that I never missed an opportunity to take a young lady on a walk down by the water.

"The Monkey Bridge Incident" is a tale that addresses that time when a boy doesn't know whether to hold hands with a girl or pull her pigtails. It's that awkward interlude between childhood and manhood that drives the best of us to do foolish things first and regret them later. How long this period lasts is relative. While one is going through this period, it can seem interminable, however the redeeming feature is that most of us still have enough child within not to let romantic tribulations bother us too much or too long.

The Monkey Bridge Incident

Sometimes the experience you have with your first girlfriend is like discovering there was poison ivy in the watermelon patch. You wonder if getting ahold of those melons was worth all the itching. Now, this isn't a story about my first girlfriend. It's a story about a certain instance that involved Eustace Barlow and his first girlfriend. You might ask, why not a story about me? The fact is, it wasn't until I was older that I even got near the watermelon patch, so this wouldn't be much of a story if I was writing about my experiences. There was this time with Eustace, though, that makes a right good telling.

It happened when I was about 11 or so, which was a long time ago. So long ago, I have probably forgotten just how much time has passed. Let's just say it happened while Dwight David Eisenhower was president. If you don't know when that was, just check it out on the interweb. I tried it, and according to the computer, I got 1,880,000 results in 0.36 seconds. Pretty doggone fast, I would say, and I bet you could figure it out from there.

I didn't live in a neighborhood. I lived along a sleepy little stream. There were several other families living along the same creek as well as in the general vicinity. Naturally, there was a bunch of us kids all about the same age. Back then, we would have said we played together almost all the time. Now, I guess we'd say we spent all our time hanging out.

If you had a creek handy, that's where you spent your time in the summer. There was a whole art to spending time at the creek. You could paddle around on a homemade raft, wade along the bank, skip stones, race sticks under the bridge, catch crawdads, not to mention fishing.

One summer morning, Shorty Evans, Buzzy Riesman, Pudgy Lumpkins, Eustace Barlow, and I were sitting on the bank pitching walnuts at a red ball that was floating by. After the ball moved along out of range, I suggested we see how long we could stand on one leg in the water. All of us, except Eustace, started to remove one sneaker.

"Why aren't you taking off your sneaker?" Shorty asked.

"I don't want to get wet," Eustace grumbled.

"What's the matter Useless? Mommy gonna spank you if you get in the creek?" Buzzy taunted. Eustace glared back.

"As a matter of fact, I don't care to get wet today," Eustace snipped.

"Suit yourself," said Buzzy.

Sitting on the edge of the bank, we stretched one barefoot leg out as far as possible over the water. Then, using a stick to push away from the bank, we stood upright in the water on our bare foot, holding the other high and dry. Buzzy and I held on to our sticks using them for balance like the tightrope walking Wallendas. This immediately elicited cries of 'no fair' from Shorty and Pudgy. We didn't have time to respond, because Pudgy, not known for his athletic ability, began to rock back and forth, desperately seeking his equilibrium. To no avail, down he crashed, sending a small tsunami rolling out across the creek.

The redeeming factor of falling in a creek is that the water serves as a cushion. Consequently, the only thing hurt was Pudgy's pride. Needless to say, we laughed so hard that soon, each of us had a wet sneaker, so we sloshed over to Pudgy and helped him up.

We were drying on the bank when Shorty blurted, "We ought to build a monkey bridge."

"A what?" asked Buzzy.

"A monkey bridge, ya' dope," came Shorty's reply.

"I heard you the first time, but what is it?"

"It's a bridge, you know, to cross something, like the creek."

"We got one up there," I said, pointing to the two-lane concrete car bridge.

"And we got the old footbridge down there," Eustace said, pointing in the opposite direction. "What do we need another one for?"

"I prefer the concrete bridge," said Pudgy.

"To get over to the island, dummies," Shorty shot back, ignoring Pudgy.

We all sat in silence as we pondered what Shorty had said. Down beyond the footbridge, a squat dam sat at the lower end of the creek, forming a large pool that we called the 'lake.' About midway between, years of silt and sediment deposits had created a small island. Hardly bigger than a green on a par 9 golf course, and overgrown with weeds, brush, and a tree or two, the island called to us. A mere 10 feet separated it from our side of the shore. On the other side, it was a good 25 feet to the bank. We had been on the island a few times, when we could "borrow" a boat. But as for unfettered access, we were stymied. A bridge opened all sorts of possibilities.

"I'm in," I said.

"Me too," chimed in Buzzy.

Eustace shrugged his shoulders.

We looked at Pudgy. He had just tucked a Goo Goo Cluster in his mouth and all he could do was nod and chew.

"Do you know how to build a monkey bridge?" Buzzy asked Shorty.

"Of course I do," he said emphatically, "I was up to the Scout-O-Rama last weekend to see my cousin Clifford compete in a fire startin' contest. While I was there, I watched a bunch of 'em put up a monkey bridge. Nothin' to it. All's you need is a couple of poles and some rope."

"That doesn't sound too difficult," I said. "We could knock that out in no time. What do we need?"

"Well, like I said," Shorty huffed, "we need some poles, rope and the like."

"How big, how many and how much?' Buzzy asked.

"Give me a minute," Shorty said, rubbing his scalp like he was kneading a dough ball. "Come on," was all he said, and walked off down the creek bank.

We followed him in silence until we reached a spot directly across from the island. "Are we all on board?" Shorty asked.

"Yeah," shouted Buzzy.

"Sure," I added.

"I guess," muttered Eustace

"MmmmMmmm," was the only sound that came from Pudgy.

"Was that a 'yes' or are you eatin' something?" Shorty asked, scowling at Pudgy.

"MmmmMmmm."

"I'll take that as a 'yes'. Now, we need three pieces of thick rope that can reach across the creek with about ten feet to spare on each end. We'll also need four poles about as thick as your leg and at least eight feet long. Then we need some thinner rope for lashing and stringers. How's about you and Buzzy going and finding the poles," Shorty said, pointing a finger at our noses. "Me and Useless will work on the rope. Bring anything else you can find that will be useful. We'll meet back here after lunch. OK?"

"I can't make any promises," said Eustace.

"What, you got something better to do?" I asked.

"Well, maybe," Eustace replied sheepishly.

"Wouldn't involve a certain redhead would it?" Buzzy teased.

"Shaddup! It's none of your business," Eustace snapped, cheeks turning crimson. He turned and stomped off. We watched him in silence for a little while as he headed off toward the two-lane, before turning our attention back to the business at hand. None of us had picked up on the significance of Buzzy's question.

"What about Pudgy?" I asked. He had remained silent during the entire conversation.

Shorty contemplated my question for a moment or two, then said, "We'll put him in charge of snacks." He turned to Pudgy and asked, "That OK with you?"

Pudgy smiled, revealing two rows of teeth chocked full of peanuts and caramel. "Thought you'd never ask," he answered. Then, he used his pinky finger to gouge a wad of nougat loose from his molars. He examined it as a diamond cutter would a raw diamond, then swiftly returned it to his mouth with a flick of his tongue.

"Alright then," Shorty said, "see y'all after lunch."

So, we set off to do some scavenging. Buzzy and I headed up to the woods behind my house. There was always a tree or two down and we figured that would be the best place to find some poles. We found two good trees that had come down but they were too long for us to handle. I ran back to the shed and brought back a hatchet and a saw. Buzzy whacked off the limbs while I spent the better part of an hour cutting the poles down to size. After we lugged them down to the creek, we barely had time for some lunch.

Everyone appeared back at the creek about the same time. Funny how, back then, we could tell time without a watch or a cell phone. We took inventory of all the stuff we had found. There were the poles Buzzy and I had brought. Shorty had trudged up pulling a battered old Radio Flyer wagon filled with rope and an inflatable raft.

He said he planned to float across on the raft rather than slog through all the muck that lined the bottom of the creek. Buzzy showed up with some old clothesline and a mallet. I brought the saw and hatchet which I had dragged down the hill in the old washtub that hung on the back of our shed. Pudgy ambled up with a threadbare pillow case filled with goodies in one hand and a carton of Nehi cream soda in the other. We figured there was half again as much stuff hidden away in Pudgy's pockets.

We were busy taking inventory when Eustace showed up. You could have knocked us over with a feather. He was being led along by Margaret Mary Butts. All activity stopped. She walked right up to us, Eustace in tow. She abruptly stopped and gave Eustace a dig in the ribs with her elbow. "Hi y'all, you know Margaret, don't ya?" Eustace asked timidly. No one said a word.

We all knew Margaret Mary Butts from school. Most everybody referred to her as Little Red. She didn't like that nickname, though, and it was worth your life if she heard you utter it. She was Little Red because her mom was Big Red. They both had fiery red hair, blue eyes and more freckles than ants at a picnic. A rangy, but amply endowed woman, Big Red Butts was the star pitcher for the Buechel Belles, a local softball team. They had been undefeated for the past three years. Big Red had been Moira Mahoney in high school, earning her nickname as a standout cheerleader and track star. She and her future husband, Thornton Butts, had been sweethearts all through school. Thorton, known as Mighty Thor because of his football heroics, went to college on a scholarship but left after 3 seasons of bench warming to marry Big Red and open Thor Butts's Used Cars.

"I also brought some baling wire and a pair of side cutters." Eustace added, avoiding our bewildered stares.

After a few awkward moments of silence, Shorty said, "Hey, Margaret, what brings you out today?"

"Eustace said you were building a bridge and he invited me to help," came her reply.

"Oh, he did," shot back Shorty, casting a sideways look at Eustace. "That was nice of him, we were hoping he'd do that. You sure you're up to the task? It might mean getting a little dirty and maybe wet."

"She'll be OK," Eustace blurted out before Little Red could say anything. He looked at her with big moon eyes, "Don't worry, they'll do all the gettin' dirty."

"Well, it's settled then," said Shorty, "Let's get busy."

Since Shorty was the only one of us who had actually seen a monkey bridge, it fell to him to organize and direct the work. His plan was fairly straightforward. Lash the poles together to form two X shaped frames. One would stand on each bank. Stretch three ropes from bank to bank. Position two ropes, one on either side of the frames, and one over the intersections. Tie off the outer ropes to the ends of the frames, being careful to ensure each one was the same length. Shorty said they were the hand ropes. Tie a piece of Buzzy's clothesline to each frame end to tie off and steady the frames when raised. Once the frames were standing and tied off, the center rope would be stretched tight and pegged down somewhere behind the frame. Shorty said the center rope was the foot rope. According to Shorty, once everything was tied off, the monkey bridge would be fully operational and we could walk along the foot rope high and dry using the hand ropes for balance.

It sounded like a good plan to us. Shorty and Buzzy took turns floating over to the island on the raft, pulling their supplies along in the washtub. I tied some sticks to the ropes and floated them across the creek. Pudgy checked and rechecked the goodies and managed to help me out a little. Little Red flitted around, complaining about the bugs and heat. She also constantly distracted Eustace. Each time she 'eeked', he would leave whatever he was doing and head straight for her. It was impossible to keep him on a task. Pudgy and I eventually gave up and let him follow Little Red around.

Work stopped midafternoon for a snack. Pudgy had been assailing the contents of his pillowcase since we started. Consequently, what was left for us to share was meager, at best. It was too hot to eat much anyway, so I don't think anyone really minded. We did, however, get to enjoy the cream sodas which we had put in the creek to keep cold. After downing the sweet concoction, work resumed.

It was getting on in the afternoon when we finished tying off the last of the ropes. Except for Little Red and Eustace, grime and sweat filled every nook and cranny of our bodies. We gazed at our engineering wonder. It glowed in the afternoon sun.

"Who's gonna be first?" I shouted across the water to Shorty.

"Wait 'till we get over there before we decide," Shorty called back.

We gathered to decide who would receive the honor of crossing first.

"Shorty ought to go first," I said. "After all, it was his idea in the first place."

"You got a point there," Buzzy agreed.

While we were talking, Little Red had collared Eustace, whispering something in his ear. Eustace hung his head. Just as Shorty was opening his mouth to respond, Little Red gave Eustace a sharp thump in the arm. He immediately blurted out, "I think Margaret should go first. After all, isn't it ladies first?"

"That may be true for restaurants and church, Useless, but I think the honor should go to someone who actually did some work," Buzzy snarled.

"Don't call him Useless!" Little Red shouted, knotting her hand into a fist. "He did more work than you."

"Sez who?" growled Buzzy, stepping right up to Little Red, who towered over him by at least a foot.

"Hey, Hey, no need for that," I said quickly, before things escalated and Buzzy got the beating of his life. "Let's think this out. Now, we haven't tested the bridge yet. We don't know what will happen first time someone tries to cross it. Eustace, surely you wouldn't want Margaret to cross over until we make sure the bridge is safe?"

We could see the wheels turning in his head. "Well, no," he responded hesitantly.

"Eustace!" Margaret growled.

"Useless," Shorty taunted under his breath. Margaret took a step in his direction.

"Then it's settled," I said, quickly stepping between the two, "Shorty will go over first, just to make sure it's safe, then who cares who goes next? Whaddya say?"

"Well, OK, as long as Margaret goes next," Eustace agreed, keeping his head down, avoiding Little Red's glare.

"Yeah, yeah, yeah," sputtered Shorty as he backed off, glaring at Eustace.

We negotiated the rest of the crossing order while Shorty worked his way across. Reaching the other side, he raised his arms in victory and beckoned us to follow. From the get-go, some of us began to question if Shorty had remembered all the necessary aspects of monkey bridge construction. The frames wobbled with each step taken, and as more crossings were made, the foot and hand ropes began to sag. Nonetheless, the sheer thrill of crossing a monkey bridge we had made with our own hands did not deter us from going back and forth as the afternoon wore on. The footrope was almost to the water by the time I made my third round trip, leaving Shorty, Eustace and Little Red behind on the island. We had decided to try and tighten the ropes before anymore crossings were attempted.

As I set foot on terra firma, Little Red commenced to hop and shriek like she had stepped in a ground hornets' nest. Then, quite unexpectedly, amidst all the hoopla, she proceeded to peel off her top giving us a good look at the white cotton training bra she was wearing. There was no more to be seen than would be revealed at the public swimming pool. Nonetheless, the fact that we were looking at Little Red's training bra mesmerized us. All we could do was stare at her, mouths agape. After she realized our eyes were riveted on her, or more correctly, on her training bra, she stopped her hooting and hollering. What we hadn't seen, that we found out later from Shorty, who saw the whole thing up close and personal, was that unbeknownst to Little Red, Eustace had captured a grasshopper. He held it cupped between his hands. When he opened them to show Little Red, the critter jumped straight down her blouse. That explained why she then took a mighty swing at Eustace, screaming, "Useless, I'm gonna kill you!" In one amazing athletic move, Eustace ducked under her freckled fist and leaped to the monkey bridge, where he proceeded to dance along the sagging ropes, toes dipping to the water. Fortunately for him, Little Red stopped long enough to retrieve her blouse before following him, as there was no doubt the bridge would not have sustained the weight of the two of them running along together.

Little Red was approaching the halfway point, as Eustace reached our side of the bank. He planted a foot on the frame and jumped to the ground, pushing himself along by placing a hand squarely in Pudgy's chest. Having just lifted a bag of Sugar Babies to his mouth, Pudgy didn't see Eustace's hand and hadn't prepared himself to absorb its force. He toppled backward, plopping full force down on the end of the footrope, immediately taking up all the slack, propelling Little Red straight up. She tumbled, head over heels, landing with a huge splash in the middle of the creek. There she sat, up to her training bra, in swirling, muddy water.

Boys being boys, we broke out in raucous laughter. Not Eustace of course; he was hightailing it out of sight. Little Red scrambled out of the creek while we savored the sight. By now, Eustace had covered a good amount of ground. Little Red stopped long enough to tug her shirt over her head before lighting out after him. We watched them until they disappeared around the big curve on Watterson Trail.

Pudgy had put the finishing touches on the monkey bridge for sure. By now, the footrope sagged deep in the water and the frames listed precariously. Rather than risk a bridge crossing, Shorty asked us to send the raft across. It was almost supper time by the time Shorty was safely back with us. We sat on the bank for a bit while he filled us in on what had happened on the island. Knowing it was Eustace who had set things in motion made the memories even sweeter.

The following day, we didn't have the desire to try and resurrect the bridge. We wanted to preserve the moment for a while longer, savoring the previous day's events, laughing harder at each retelling, embellishing the story until it reached legendary proportions.

A good rain always seems to set things right. That night, a storm came up and the rushing water scoured the creek clean, carrying away the remains of the monkey bridge.

37

As for Eustace and Little Red, that romance didn't last through the end of the week, as so often happens with first loves. Whether it was due to Eustace losing interest or Little Red losing patience is a matter of conjecture. He never mentioned the monkey bridge incident or what happened with Little Red, despite our many attempts to find out.

It's safe to say, this experience didn't keep any of us out of the watermelon patch. On the contrary, each of us suffered at least one case of poison ivy. A couple of us got it more than once. I guess there's no overestimating the allure of watermelons.

End

Looking Back: Reflection Three

My Creek[3]

When I close my eyes,
The memory of my creek flows fiercely
Through the cataracts of my mind.
The bustle of its clear water fills my ears
With the rush of getting where it's going - and fast.

Burnished stones push their shaven heads
Above Fall's parched stream,
Forming slippery pathways from bank to bank,
Tantalizing the sure of foot to cross.
Cold feet splash in puddles at its edges
Crawdads back under rocks to hide
From curious hands.

Winter bonfires glow along the bank.
Ice skating till dark,
Then, hot chocolate and marshmallows.

My creek swells with the Spring rains
Rushing out from its banks,
Filling the bottom with muddy water,
The color of my Grandmother's coffee.
Bluegill and catfish gather in the pools,
Waiting for bait dangled from old cane poles.

---

[3] "My Creek" appeared online in *Young Ravens Literary Review: A Biannual Online Literary Journal* Issue 4 – Spring 2016

Feet dangle in the cool bath on a hot Summer's day,
Between innings played on a makeshift field,
Laid out with hats in the hollow nearby.
Mulberry and sycamore trees form the nave,
Branches stretching out across the water,
Sunlight breaking through
The stained glass mosaic of their leaves.

Now, I stare down at my creek,
Prodded and pushed to make room,
For streets and roads, houses and restaurants.
Nothing more than a drainage ditch of progress.
How old I feel.

About The Author

Paul Stansbury is a life long native of Kentucky. Now retired, he lives in Danville, Kentucky. His novelette, *Little Green Men?,* was published as a Kindle edition by Bards and Sages Publishing. His stories have appeared in the anthologies, *Brief Grislys*, published by Apocryphile Press, *Neo-Legends To Last A Deathtime* published by KY Story, *Frightening* published by SEZ Publishing, *Out of the Cave* published by MacKenzie Publishing, *In Media Res, Stories From the In-Between* published by Writespace Houston and *Nocturnal Natures* published by Zimbell House Publishing. His work has also appeared in a variety of online publications. His poetry has appeared in The Rising Phoenix Review, Young Ravens Literary Review and Kentucky Monthly.

He is a contributing writer for the Danville Advocate Messenger Newspaper. He frequently reads his work in public. He is the Scheduling Coordinator for Historic Penn's Store Annual Kentucky Writers Celebration. He is Box Office Manger and member of the Board of Directors of Scarlet Cup Theater.

Down By The Creek – Ripples And Reflections is Paul Stansbury's first book to be published.

Sheppard Press